VICTORIA'S ABC ADVENTURE

by
Cathy Warren

illustrated by
Patience Brewster

Lothrop, Lee & Shepard Books • New York

Library of Congress Cataloging in Publication Data. Warren, Cathy.   Victoria's ABC adventure. Summary: A little brown snake saves her family after pandemonium at a cookout endangers their lives. Letters of the alphabet are highlighted. [1. Snakes—Fiction. 2. Alphabet] I. Brewster, Patience, ill. II. Title. III. Title: Victoria's ABC adventure. PZ7.W2514Vi   1984   [E]   83-14847   ISBN 0-688-02021-6   ISBN 0-688-02023-2 (lib. bdg.)

For my grandmothers,
Anise Bellinger and Gail Bair.

—C.W.

To Josephine Montgomery Gregg,
who so often saves the day.

—P.B.

Every summer, Mama Snake has twenty-six babies.
They're always girls.
They're always green.

And every year, she names her babies:
a b c d e f g
h i j k l m n o p
q r s t u v
w x y and **z.**
It's always the same.

This year, Mama Snake had twenty-six babies.
"Naturally," she nodded.
They were all girls.
"Of course," she smiled.
But they weren't all green.

"You're kidding," she gasped.
"No kidding!" said a little brown snake.
She had v's down her back
and a tail that went *cha-cha-cha*.
"Who are you?" Mama asked.
"I'm Victoria," the brown snake said.

Every day, Mama taught her babies to hide, coil, and slide down rows of soft garden dirt.

The twenty-five green girls darted under lettuce leaves.
They wrapped themselves into little circles.
They slid down each row, leaving twenty-five little S tracks behind.

"You're good garden snakes," Mama said proudly.
But Victoria shook her tail
and zigzagged this way and that.

She stretched all the way out into a long line.
Then she slid across each row
and erased every single track.

"You're different, but you're special," Mama told her.

This made the green girls angry.

"She's stupid," said some.   "She's strange," said others.

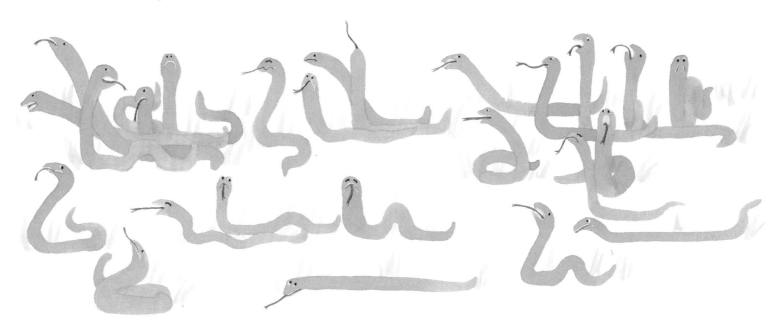

"We don't want her to be our sister," they all agreed.

This made Victoria sad.

She slid **a**way across the garden,
into a yard, and under a **b**arbecue grill.
Soon a big **c**rowd gathered for a cook-out.

That **d**ay dozens of people came to **e**at.
Each carried **f**oot-long hotdogs and put them on the **g**rill.

As the grill got **h**otter and hotter,
the hotdogs began to sizzle.
Victoria heard the hissing sound.
"Hello, snakes," she called.

Victoria **i**nched her way onto the table,

slid past the **j**uice, and bumped into a jar
that **k**nocked over a catsup bottle.
She hid inside a **l**ong bun.

A lady picked the bun up,
squirted **m**ustard on Victoria's head,
and said, "This one's mine."

"I'll just have a **n**ibble,"
the lady said.
"Ouch, **o**uch!" Victoria squealed.

She **p**opped out of the bun and into the grass.
"It's alive!" cried the lady.
People panicked.

They hurried to the pool, dove into the water, and swam **q**uickly to the **r**ubber **s**ea serpent with the x's down its back.

"Hold on **t**ight," said some.
"Snakes can't touch **u**s here," said others.

But when Victoria saw the sea serpent, she said, "Oh, there's my real sister!"

She slipped into the pool and swam underwater.

When Victoria reached the sea serpent, she kissed it so har[d] the **v**alve flew open and air **w**hooshed out.

Every **x** on the sea serpent got smaller as it shrank.
People fell off with a splash!
Victoria slipped back into the **y**ard and **z**igzagged this way and that.

People were angry.
"You've ruined our cook-out!" cried some.
"After her!" yelled others.
Victoria slid into the garden,
 shaking her tail and crying, "Danger, danger!"

Mama Snake and the twenty-five green girls
darted under the lettuce leaves.
They wrapped themselves into little circles to hide.
But Victoria stretched all the way out into a
long line and erased every single track.

Soon the crowd gathered.
"Check the garden for snake tracks," said some.
"Nothing here but lettuce and this old stick," said others.
Away they went.

"Victoria, you've saved us," Mama said proudly.
"You're smart," said some of her sisters.
"And special," said others.

"Then you want me to be your sister?"
Victoria asked.
"Naturally," they nodded.
"Of course," they smiled.

And they slid **a**
b
c
d
e
f
g
h
i
j
k
l
m
n
o
p
q
r
s
t
u
v
w
x
y
and **z** down rows of soft garden dirt.

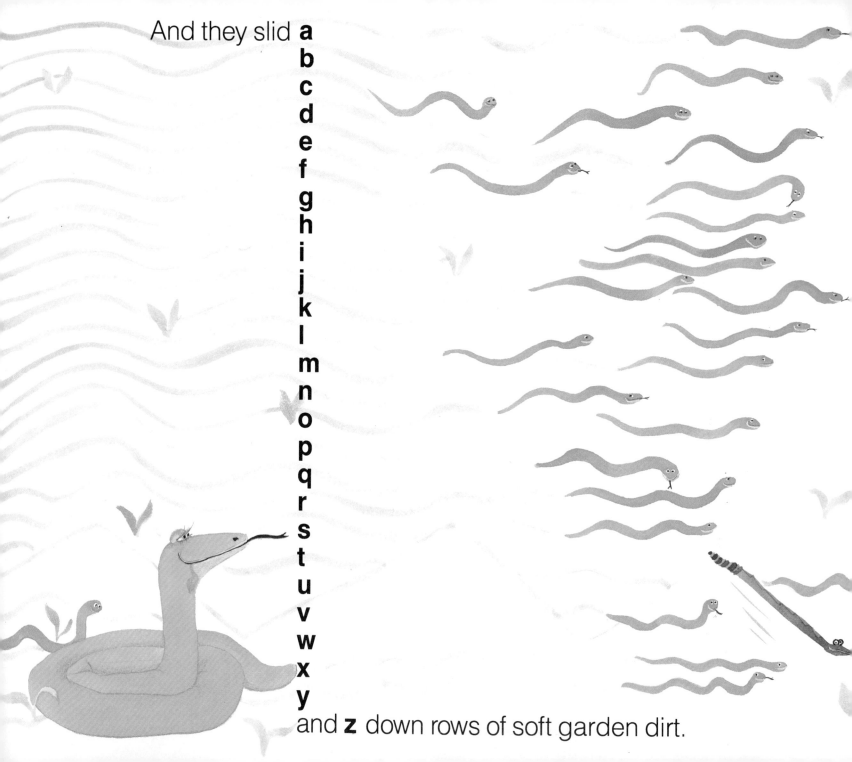